The Little Green Dragon Steps Out

Reprinted by arrangement with Hyperion Books for Children.

Text and illustrations © 1992 by Klaus Baumgart.
All rights reserved. Printed in the United States of America. © 1990 by Breitschopf
Wien-Stuttgart. First published 1990 by hpt-Verlagsgesellschaft mbH. & Co. KG,
Vienna. First published in the United States of America by Hyperion Books for
Children, 114 Fifth Avenue, New York, New York 10011.

First Hyperion Paperback edition: September 1994
1   3   5   7   9   10   8   6   4   2

Library of Congress Cataloging-in-Publication Data

Baumgart, Klaus.   [Wirklich wahr. English]   The little green dragon steps out/
Klaus Baumgart — 1st ed.   p.   cm.   Translation of: Wirklich wahr. Summary:
Anna's little green dragon comes out of her picture book and plays around her
room during the night, but was it just a dream?   ISBN 1-56282-254-3 (trade) —
ISBN 1-56282-255-1 (lib. bdg.)   ISBN 0-7868-1006-8 (pbk.) [1. Dragons —
Fiction. 2. Dreams — Fiction.] I. Title. PZ7.B3285Li   1992 [E] — dc20
92-5120   CIP   AC

The Little Green Dragon Steps Out

Klaus Baumgart

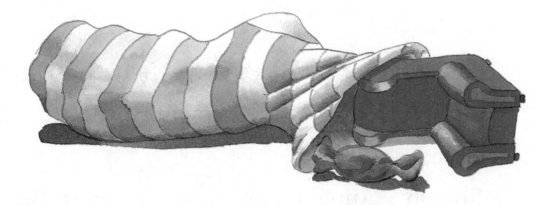

Hyperion Paperbacks for Children
New York

Anna's favorite color is green—because green is the color of the little dragon in her favorite bedtime storybook.

Tonight, Anna reads until she feels sleepy. Then, with a big sigh, she closes her book and falls asleep.

Suddenly, the pages of Anna's book start to rustle and crinkle. Out pops the Little Green Dragon, onto the blanket.

The Little Green Dragon waddles over to the window and jumps up onto the sill. He gazes for a long time at the shiny, starry night.

When he jumps down from the window…

...he slips on a marble and slides smack into something big and soft.

"Grrrr!" he hears. But Anna's teddy bear couldn't *really* have growled, so the Little Green Dragon says, "Grrrr!" right back.

Across the room, he sees a pile of doll's clothes heaped in the corner. "I *must* have those clothes!" the dragon declares.

He hops onto a roller skate and takes a wild ride to the opposite side of the bedroom.

Admiring himself in his new outfit, the dragon exclaims, "I sure am handsome!"

Pleased with himself, the Little Green Dragon struts across the bedroom to Anna's dollhouse. There he sees a cozy easy chair.

"What a comfortable chair!" he exclaims, as he settles in.

After a short rest, the Little Green Dragon leaps out of the chair and starts to fill one of Anna's socks with toys from around her room.

The Little Green Dragon drags the overflowing sock back up to Anna's bed. He makes his way to his book, throws open its cover…and dives back into his world.

The next morning, a ray of sunlight tickles Anna's nose. She wakes up and opens her book.

"Oh!" Anna gasps. She can't believe her eyes.

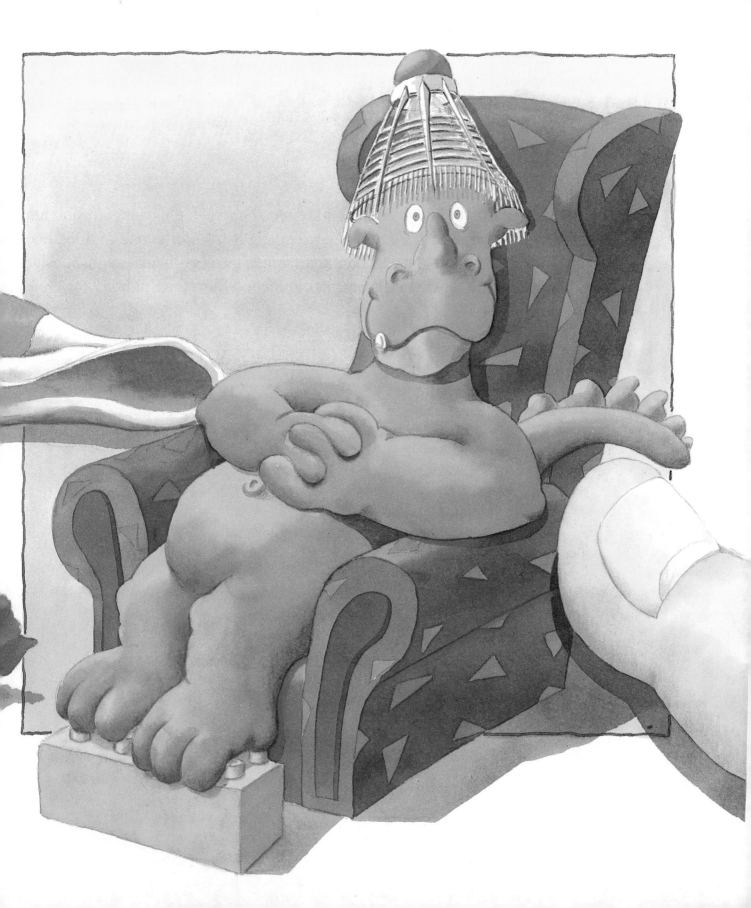

Klaus Baumgart imagined the Little Green Dragon for his daughter and number one critic, Lorraine. *The Little Green Dragon Steps Out* is one of three books about Anna and her dragon. Mr. Baumgart works as a free-lance graphic designer in Berlin, Germany, where he also creates animated films for children.